Fun in the Sun

Farmer Claude and Farmer Maude
looked at the clouds and sighed,
"For ninety days and ninety nights,
the sky has wept and cried."

They were sick of the rain.

They were sick of the hail.

They were sick of the storms.

They were sick of the gales.

"Where is the sun?" they wailed.

3

"What should we do?"
cried Farmer Claude.

"Let's find the sun!"

cried Farmer Maude.

So Farmer Claude and Farmer Maude
went to find the sun.

The dog, the goat, the rooster, and pig came along for the sun and the fun.

They drove up the hills

and down the hills

on highways and byways and trails.

They drove through the city

and then through the town

through tunnels and bridges with rails.

Then Farmer Claude and Farmer Maude
parked near the beach ahead.

"The surf, the sand, the shells, and sun will be so much fun," they said.

Farmer Claude and Farmer Maude

walked east in the afternoon.

They each built a sandcastle down by the sea

and swam in the blue lagoon.

The dog, the goat, the rooster, and pig
walked west in the afternoon.

But something followed them all the way,
a thunderous black typhoon!

The shivering animals looked at the sky,

"Where is the sun?" they wailed.

The typhoon grew blacker over their heads.

It started to rain, then it hailed.

The dog, the goat, the rooster, and pig

ran back to the blue lagoon.

But something followed them all the way,

a miserable wet monsoon!

The poor wet animals got back on the truck.

"Oh, where was the sun?" they sighed.

The sand was sticking to all of their feet,

and they couldn't get dry though they tried.

21

Farmer Claude and Farmer Maude

got into the front of the truck.

"Now that was a day that we'll never forget.

We've really had wonderful luck!"

Farmer Claude and Farmer Maude

looked back at the beach and smiled.

"There was sand, there was sea,

there was plenty of sun,

and the weather was marvellously mild."

The dog, the goat, the rooster, and pig

looked back at the beach with alarm.

"There was sand, there was sea,

but where was the sun?

We should have stayed back on the farm!"